D0996353

The Twelve
Dancing Princesses

The Twelve
Dancing Princesses

Jane Ray
after the brothers Grimm

ORCHARD BOOKS

for my sisters Elizabeth and Caroline, with much love

Orchard Books

96 Leonard Street, London EC2A 4RH

Orchard Books Australia

14 Mars Road, Lane Cove, NSW 2066

First published in Great Britain in 1996

Illustrations © Jane Ray 1996

The right of Jane Ray to be identified as the Illustrator

of this Work has been asserted by her in accordance

with the Copyright, Designs and Patents Act, 1988.

A CIP catalogue record for this book is available

from the British Library.

1 85213 997 8

Printed in Belgium

There was once a king who had twelve daughters, each one as clever and beautiful as the next. He loved them all dearly but was puzzled by a mystery that happened night after night.

Every evening the king would tenderly kiss his daughters and settle them down to sleep in the long bedchamber they shared. He then tiptoed out, always taking care to lock and bolt the door behind him.

Yet every morning the princesses were tired and wan and their silken shoes were danced to pieces. Where did they go each night? And how did they leave their room? The king was determined to solve the mystery. For one thing twelve new pairs of dancing slippers a day was costing him a fortune.

The princesses were certainly not telling, so the king issued a proclamation. Any man who could discover their secret would marry one of the princesses and rule the kingdom with her on the old king's death. But he must find the answer in three days and three nights or be banished from the kingdom forever.

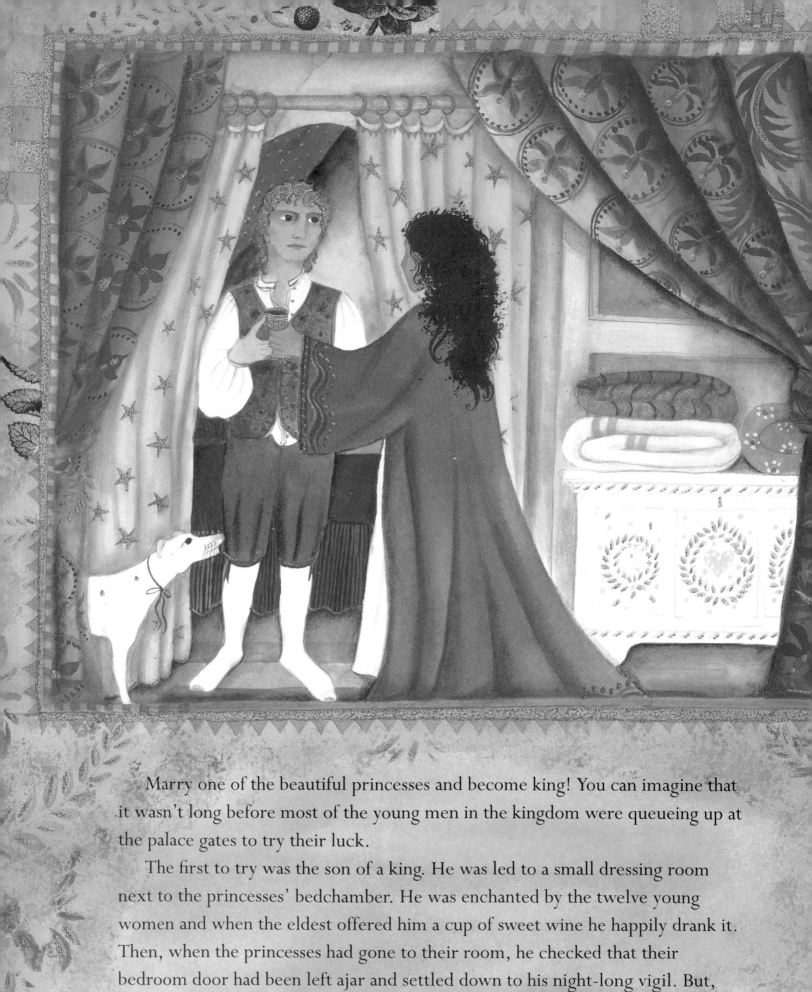

Marry one of the beautiful princesses and become king! You can imagine that it wasn't long before most of the young men in the kingdom were queueing up at the palace gates to try their luck.

The first to try was the son of a king. He was led to a small dressing room next to the princesses' bedchamber. He was enchanted by the twelve young women and when the eldest offered him a cup of sweet wine he happily drank it. Then, when the princesses had gone to their room, he checked that their bedroom door had been left ajar and settled down to his night-long vigil. But, however hard he struggled, the prince could not keep his eyes open. He was

overcome by asleep and suddenly it was morning. There in their beds were the
twelve princesses, sleeping soundly, and there on the floor were the twelve
pairs of worn-out slippers, the evidence of his failure.

The second night, the same sweet wine, the same overwhelming need to
sleep and the same failure. And again the third night. The young prince was
duly banished from the kingdom and another suitor took up the challenge.

And so it continued. The king was in despair. Were his daughters able to
outwit every man in the kingdom?

Some time later a poor soldier, returning wounded from a battle in a faraway country, sat down to rest by the side of the road. He was enjoying his simple meal of bread and cheese when an old woman approached and, because the soldier was a kind man, he offered her half his lunch.

"Where are you heading?" the old woman asked. The soldier laughed. "Off to try my luck at the palace", he said. "I could quite fancy being king!"

But the old woman remained serious. "Don't touch the wine those clever girls offer you. Just pretend to drink, then pretend to fall asleep. And if you wear this cloak, you'll become invisible and be able to follow them wherever they go."

The soldier was puzzled, but he thanked the strange old woman, took the cloak, and set off for the palace.

By now the king had given up hope of solving his daughters' secret,
but he greeted the soldier courteously. And so, when bedtime came, the
soldier was led to the small room next to the princesses' bedchamber.
The eldest princess offered him a cup of wine and the soldier pretended
to sip… and to sip some more. The wine did not run down his throat but
into a small sponge he had cleverly tied under his chin.

Then, as if overcome with tiredness, the soldier yawned loudly and rolled over onto his bed. "Silly fool," said the eldest princess. And laughing merrily, the twelve sisters danced into their room to prepare for the night ahead.

They flung open their cupboards and trunks and began to dress themselves in
fine lace and linen, embroidered silk and rich velvet and brocade. They curled
and plaited each other's hair, painted lips and powdered faces, ruffled fans and
finally every princess slipped on a new pair of dancing shoes . . .

Only the youngest could not enjoy herself. "Something feels wrong tonight,"
she said. But her eldest sister – impatient to be off – told her not to be a silly
goose, and clapped her hands three times. A door appeared in the wall and
slowly swung open and the twelve princesses disappeared.

The soldier clambered from his bed and hurried after them, flinging his magic cloak around his shoulders as he went. But in his haste he stumbled on his wounded leg and stepped on the hem of the youngest princess' dress. "What was that?" she cried. "Someone is following us. I know something's not right tonight."

"Nonsense," said her eldest sister. But the youngest sensed something all the same and kept glancing over her shoulder, as they made their way down flights of stairs and along corridors. Finally they arrived at a small wooden door. This opened out onto a garden.

The soldier drew his breath: he had never seen such a magical place.

The princesses hurried through the silvery trees, which glimmered in the moonlight.

They came to a garden of gold, where plump and delicious fruits
hung down from the branches, burnished and bronzed. Then they stepped
through an arch of roses into a third garden all of diamonds which sparkled
and shimmered in the dark like a spangled sky of stars.

In each garden the soldier felt he must be dreaming and reached up to snap off a twig, just to be sure. Each time the youngest princess was startled by the noise; and each time her sisters laughed away her fears and hurried her on.

An avenue of diamond-studded trees led down to a lake and there, on
the water, bobbed twelve little painted boats. In each sat a handsome prince,
waiting to row the princesses across the water.

The soldier, growing used to this strange and magical world by now,
climbed into the boat with the youngest princess, taking care to cover himself
completely with his invisible cloak.

After a while the little prince rowing the boat stopped to rest. "Why is the boat so slow tonight, when I'm rowing as hard as I always do?" The youngest sister only shivered in reply.

Across the lake stood a wonderful castle. Lights shone from every window, fireworks exploded in the sky above, and the sound of drums and trumpets, flutes and violins reached down to the boats, urging all to join the party.

The princesses ran up to the castle and danced with their princes all through the night. They ate the most mouthwatering of foods and drank the finest wines. The soldier, hidden safely in his cloak, danced alone, weaving amongst the couples and stealing morsels of food from under the noses of the unseeing guests. Once, feeling very bold, he took a sip from the youngest princess' goblet.

"Now someone is helping themselves to my drink," she said, almost in tears.
But her eldest sister, whirling past, only laughed at her. "Oh do stop worrying
and come and dance. We've only a few hours left."

And sure enough, their slippers were soon so worn through that they could
not be danced in a minute longer. It was time for the princesses to go home.

The princes rowed the sisters back across the lake and this time the soldier travelled with the eldest princess. All the young women were beautiful in their own ways, but she was the most interesting to him.

The princesses promised to meet their princes the following night, and hurried back through the three gardens and along the palace passageways.

They were tiring by now, and sleepily climbed the last flight of stairs. The soldier slipped past them in his cloak. And by the time the princesses peeped in through his door he was lying in his bed, apparently fast asleep and snoring gently.

"Silly fool!" yawned the eldest princess. "But our secret is still safe." And she lingered a moment, watching him as he slept.

The next morning the soldier felt sure it had all been a dream, in spite of the three twigs he had picked from the gardens. He decided to keep his vigil once more before seeing the king. The second night was exactly like the first and the soldier enjoyed himself so much he couldn't resist following the princesses for a third night of dancing and feasting. This last time he came away with a golden goblet under his cloak as further proof.

On the fourth morning, the king wearily summoned the soldier to his study. The sisters hid outside the door to hear how he would fare. "Have you discovered how my daughters wear out their slippers every night?" asked the king.

"I have, your majesty," replied the soldier. "They dance away the night in an underground castle, with twelve handsome princes." And he produced from his pockets the three twigs and the golden goblet, as he explained about the hidden door, the three gardens, the lake and the castle.

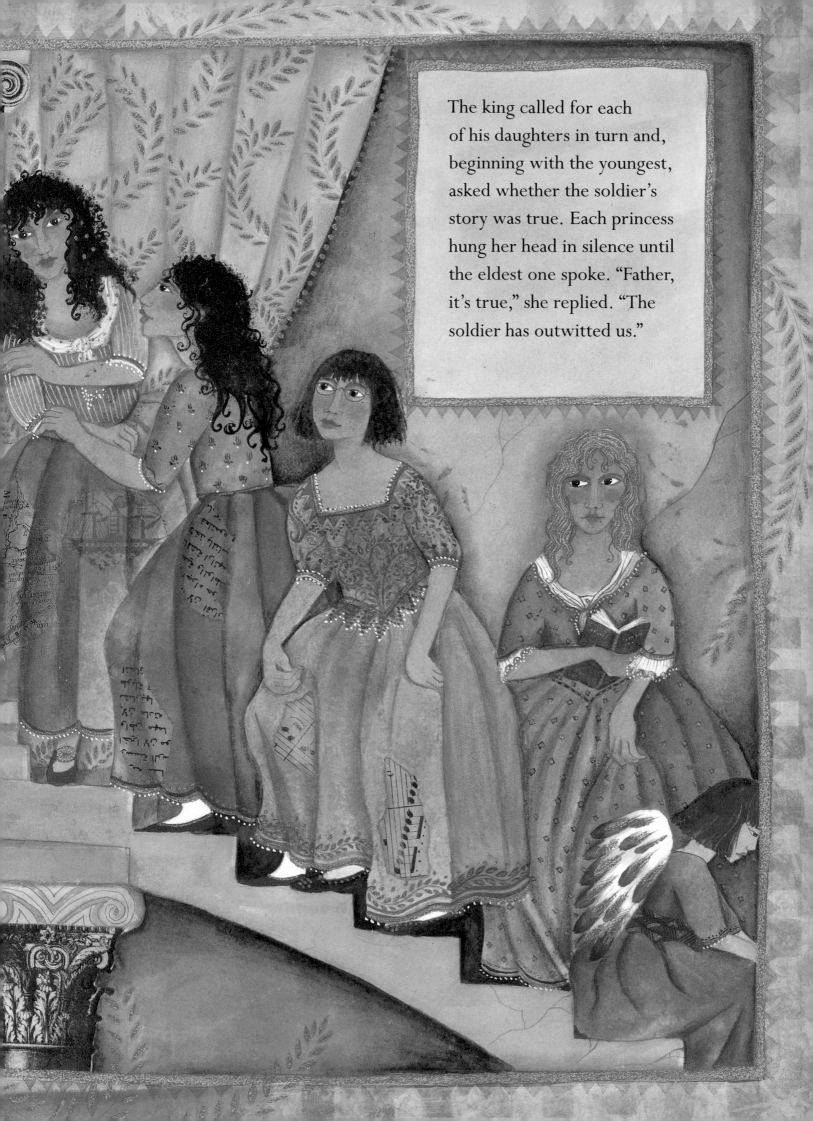

The king called for each of his daughters in turn and, beginning with the youngest, asked whether the soldier's story was true. Each princess hung her head in silence until the eldest one spoke. "Father, it's true," she replied. "The soldier has outwitted us."

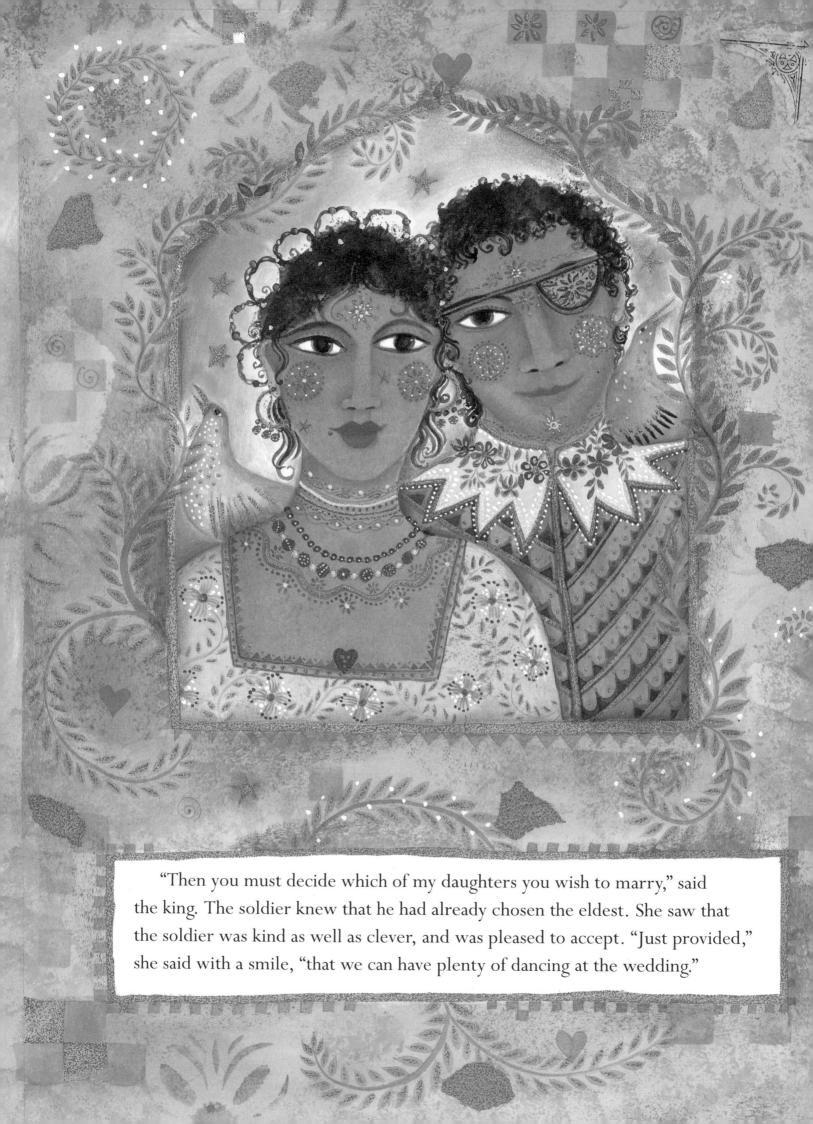

"Then you must decide which of my daughters you wish to marry," said the king. The soldier knew that he had already chosen the eldest. She saw that the soldier was kind as well as clever, and was pleased to accept. "Just provided," she said with a smile, "that we can have plenty of dancing at the wedding."

The wedding took place soon afterwards and they danced the night away.

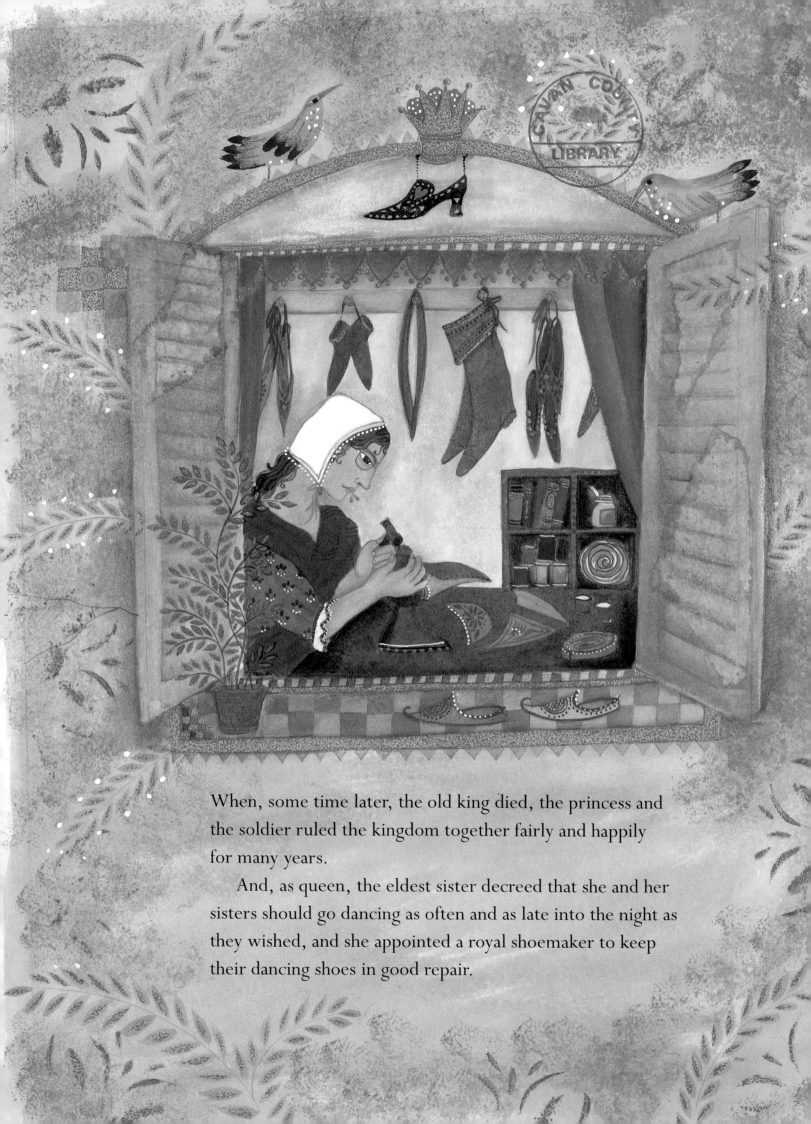

When, some time later, the old king died, the princess and the soldier ruled the kingdom together fairly and happily for many years.

And, as queen, the eldest sister decreed that she and her sisters should go dancing as often and as late into the night as they wished, and she appointed a royal shoemaker to keep their dancing shoes in good repair.